The Frog with the Big Mouth

Retold by **Teresa Bateman**   Illustrated by **Will Terry**

www.av2books.com

Your AV² Media Enhanced book gives you a fiction readalong online. Log on to www.av2books.com and enter the unique book code from this page to use your readalong.

AV² Readalong Navigation

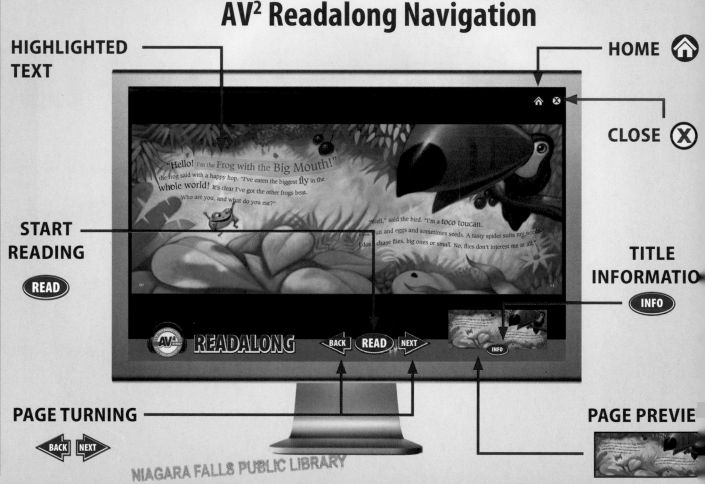

HIGHLIGHTED TEXT

HOME

CLOSE

START READING

TITLE INFORMATIO

PAGE TURNING

PAGE PREVIE

Go to **www.av2books.com**, and enter this book's unique code.

BOOK CODE

L375699

AV² by **Weigl** brings you media enhanced books that support active learning.

First Published by

ALBERT WHITMAN & COMPANY
Publishing children's books since 1919

Published by AV² by Weigl

350 5th Avenue, 59th Floor New York, NY 10118

Copyright ©2013 AV² by Weigl

052012
WEP160512

Printed in the United States of America in North Mankato, Minnesota

1 2 3 4 5 6 7 8 9 0 16 15 14 13 12

Text copyright © 2008 by Teresa Bateman. Illustrations copyright © 2008 by Will Terry.

Published in 2008 by Albert Whitman & Company

Library of Congress Cataloging-in-Publication Data

Bateman, Teresa.

The frog with the big mouth / retold by Teresa Bateman ; illustrated by Will Terry.

p. cm.

Summary: In this version of the classic folktale, an Argentine wide-mouthed frog sets out through the rain forest to brag about his fly-eating abilities and encounters a toco toucan, a coati, a capybara, and a jaguar. Includes a note about the South American rain forest animals featured in the story.

ISBN 978-1-61913-146-0 (hard cover : alk. paper)

[1. Frogs--Folklore. 2. Folklore.] I. Terry, Will, 1966- ill. II. Title.

PZ8.1.B3316Fr 2012

398.2--dc23
[E]

2012017286

Once there was a frog who lived in the rainforest by Iguazú Falls, where Argentina meets Brazil. He was a young frog, a new frog, a barely more than a polly wog frog, who was more mouth than body or brain, and still had much to learn.

One day, while eating with his family, he caught a big fly, a huge fly, an enormous fly!

4

He opened his mouth up wide, wide, **wide,** and gulped it down.

"Look at **me!**" he cried, with a braggy bounce. "I'm the Frog with the Big Mouth! I've eaten the biggest fly in the whole world. Don't you wish you were **me?**"

His brothers and sisters shrugged and kept on eating.

So the **Frog with the Big Mouth** set out to find someone else to impress.

Soon he caught sight of something with a bright orange bill and feathers. Then two eyes opened up above the orange bill and blinked at him.

"Hello! I'm the Frog with the Big Mouth!" the frog said with a happy hop. "I've eaten the biggest fly in the whole world! It's clear I've got the other frogs beat. Who are you, and what do you eat?"

"Well," said the bird. "I'm a toco toucan.
I eat fruit and eggs and sometimes seeds. A tasty spider suits my needs.
I don't chase flies, big ones or small. No, flies don't interest me at all."

11

"Too bad! Too bad!" said the Frog with the Big Mouth. "Don't you wish you were me?" And he continued down the path.

Suddenly a creature with a narrow triangular nose peeked out of a bush and sniffed at him. It had small ears, a furry body, and a long, l-o-n-g striped tail.

14

The frog was a little nervous, but that didn't stop him. "Hello! I'm the Frog with the Big Mouth!" he said with a little leap. "I've eaten the biggest fly in the whole world! I've got frogs and the toco toucan beat! Who are you, and what do you eat?"

The furry creature climbed up a nearby tree. "I'm a **coati.** I eat fruit and termites, sometimes mice. Roots and lizards are also nice. I tried flies once, if I recall. Now flies don't interest me at all."

16

"Too bad! Too bad!" said the Frog with the Big Mouth. "Don't you wish you were me?"

17

He continued along the path, looking for others to amaze. Soon he came to a pond. A head poked out of the water, then a big, brown, furry creature pulled himself onto the shore.

"Hello! I'm the Frog with the Big Mouth!" said the frog with a jubilant jump. "I've eaten the biggest fly in the whole world! I've got frogs, toco toucan, and coati beat! Who are you, and what do you eat?"

The animal shook a little water from his fur. "I'm a capybara. I eat leaves, and plants that grow in water. Grass and such are my favorite fodder. I don't eat flies, big ones or small. No, flies don't interest me at all."

"Too bad! Too bad!" said the Frog with the Big Mouth. "Don't you wish you were me?"

By now the frog was getting a little tired, but he kept hopping along, wanting to brag just a bit more before heading home.

Then he stopped. In the path something moved. It was speckled and twisty and blocking his way.

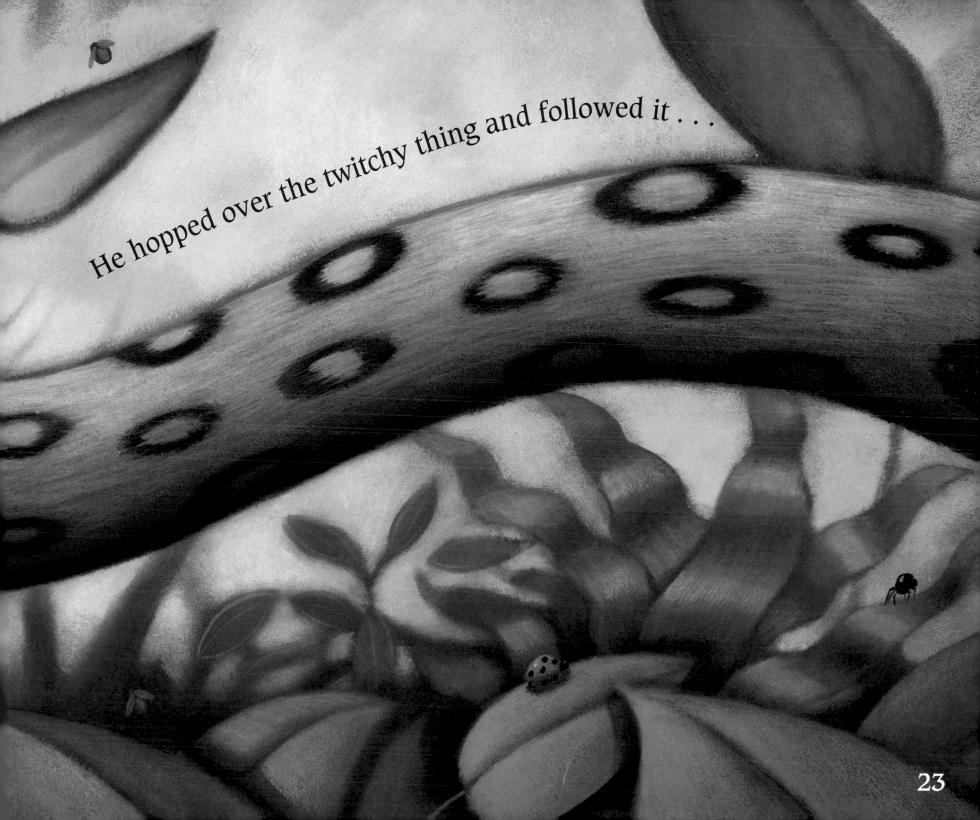

He hopped over the twitchy thing and followed it . . .

until he came to a furry spotted body and a large head that turned to look at him. The strange creature smiled, showing sharp teeth. But that didn't stop the frog.

"Hello! I'm the Frog with the Big Mouth!" he said with a saucy skip. "I've eaten the biggest fly in the whole world! I've got frogs, toco toucan, coati, and capybara beat! Who are you, and what do you eat?"

The creature stood, stretched, and his tail twitched faster. "I'm a jaguar," he purred. "Coatis and toucans are nice to chew, and I eat capybaras, too. I don't eat flies, big ones, or small. No, flies don't interest me at all. But my favorite type of chow is big-mouthed frog—

and here's one now!"

The **Frog** with the **Big Mouth** gulped and, without thinking, took a stupendous spring high, HIGH, HIGH over the jaguar's head . . .

28

and into a nearby tree.

"Look at me!" he cried. "I'm the Frog with the Big Jump! Don't you wish you were me?" He leaped from the branch, hurrying home to tell his brothers and sisters . . . and anyone else along the way.

30

About the Animals in This Book

Toco toucans are birds with large, light beaks. Found in rainforests over much of South America, they are the largest birds in the toucan family. Their beaks can be eight inches long and are deep orange with a black spot near the tip. Toco toucans have black feathers with a patch of white at the throat, edged with red. They like to eat fruit, but also feed on seeds, spiders, eggs, and an occasional lizard or bird. They also eat insects, so they might eat flies, after all.

Coatis are related to raccoons and are found in parts of North, South, and Central America. They can be up to twenty-seven inches in length with a striped tail that can be as long as their bodies. They like woodlands, desert grasslands, wet jungles, and forests. They are great climbers, and they often spend their nights in trees. They also swim well. Coatis eat fruit and, sometimes, mice, lizards, frogs, and insects . . . which would include flies.

Capybaras are the largest rodents in the world. They can be more than four feet long and more than a hundred pounds. They are excellent swimmers and can stay underwater for up to five minutes. They like to live in groups near water and eat mainly grasses and water plants. If a capybara ate a fly, it would only be by accident! Jaguars are the largest species of cat in the Western Hemisphere. They can be between five feet and eight and a half feet long (including their tails), and can weigh around eighty pounds to over three hundred pounds. Their spotted coat helps them blend in and hide. Jaguars can climb trees, and will eat just about any living creature smaller than themselves, including flies.

Argentine wide-mouthed frogs, also known as Argentine horned frogs, have an even more popular nickname—Pacman frogs! This is because of their enormous mouths, and their tendency to eat just about anything that won't eat them first. They can grow up to five and a half inches long, and their mouths are nearly as wide as their heads. Native to South America, they come in lots of colors but are most often green with red markings. Unlike the frog in the story, these frogs don't move around much—they prefer to wait for their dinner to come to them. That dinner might include insects, lizards, other frogs, and even small mammals and birds. If they can get their mouths around it, they'll try to eat it . . . and probably brag about it afterwards!

Mark on front cover inside noted Mar 10/17 BJ